— '79 | 3 7 8 0   E

DATE DUE			
JAN 18 '80			

ABOUT THE BOOK

A young Indian looks forward to his first battle, dreaming of glory as he participates in the age-old rituals of war preparation. When, fearful but excited, he joins the attack on a neighboring community, he is not prepared for the horror that surrounds him as the village is burned and people are hurt and killed. The death of a young enemy before his eyes, a boy exactly like himself, sickens the young warrior. When he himself is badly wounded, he realizes bitterly that war promises not manhood, but pain and death.

Exhaustively researched, forceful drawings depict a fascinating culture, and a glossary is included to help young readers with unfamiliar terms.

a Let Me Read book

Illustrations by

Lorinda Bryan Cauley

The War Party

By WILLIAM O. STEELE

Harcourt Brace Jovanovich

HBJ   New York and London

— '79 I 3 7 8 0

Printed in the United States of America

Library of Congress Cataloging in Publication Data

Steele, William O.   1917–
     The war party.

     (A Let me read book)
     SUMMARY: Despite his preparations a young Indian
warrior's first battle is not what he expected.
     [1. Indians—Fiction.   2. War—Fiction]
     I. Cauley, Lorinda Bryan.   II. Title.
     PZ7.S8148War   [E]   78–52815
     ISBN 0–15–294789–2
     ISBN 0–15–694697–1 pbk.

First edition

B C D E F G H I J K

To
Leila and Murrey Crutcher
for their bushels of help

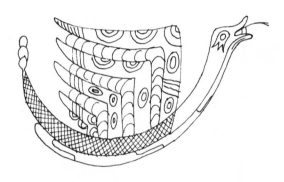

"Whoo whoop! Whoo whoop!"
The war cry rang out one afternoon.
In the Indian town, men left their houses
when they heard the cry.
They wondered who had sounded it and why.
It had been a long time since a war party
had gone from the village.

Women stopped work in their gardens.
Others were hoeing weeds
in the cornfields around the village.
They dropped their stone hoes and
hurried across the fields.
They wanted to know
if their husbands would go to war.

8

Children stopped their games
and ran toward the sound of the war cry.
"Whoo whoop! Whoo whoop!"

Not everyone in the town came
to hear the news.
Some women kept to their work of making
clay pots and sewing moccasins.

Some warriors stayed in their houses, carving.
They carved stone pipes.
They chipped and shaped small pieces of flint
into pointed arrowheads.
A brave would go to war if he wanted to go,
or he could stay at home.
He was the one to make the choice.

"Whoo whoop! Whoo whoop!"
The crowd gathered at the house
of a war chieftain.
He gave the war cry again.
Then he marched around his winter house,
a round building made of wood,
its outside plastered over with mud.
The chieftain sang a war song as he walked.
The song told of the many battles he had fought.
It told how brave he was.
It told what a great fighter he had always been.
As he sang, he beat on his drum.
Three times he circled his winter house,
singing and drumming.

Then he halted and faced the villagers.
They were his friends and his kin.
They would listen to what he had to say.
He told them that he wanted to go
on the warpath.
His younger brother had been killed
by their enemy last fall.

"Now spring has come," he said.
"The days are sunny.
The nights are warm.
It is time to raise the war club.
It is time to go against our enemy.
Our enemy will never let us live in peace.
He has always given us trouble and sorrow.
It is time we drive these hateful ones away
from their village.
My brother's ghost awaits revenge.
Then we can live in freedom from fear.
Many times I have led our warriors
against our enemies.
I have always been a good war leader."

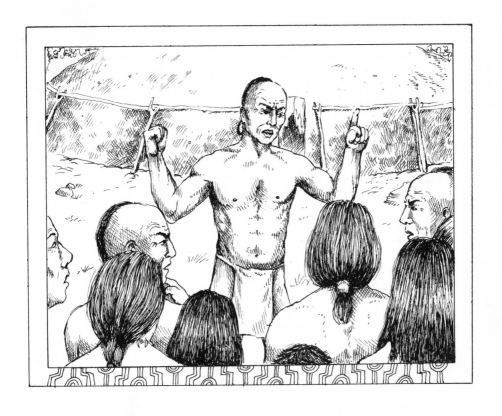

Many of the warriors nodded their heads.
The chieftain spoke the truth.
A few of the young Indians trembled
with excitement.
The words of the chieftain made them feel
strong and full of courage.
They thought how glorious it would be
to fight their first war with this great leader.

The chieftain called for warriors to join him—
warriors who were not afraid of enemy
arrows, spears, and axes.
He wanted warriors who would not run away.
He wanted followers who were braver
than the enemy.
"Whoo whoop! Whoo whoop! Whoo whoop!"
He yelled the war cries once again.
He beat his drum faster and faster.

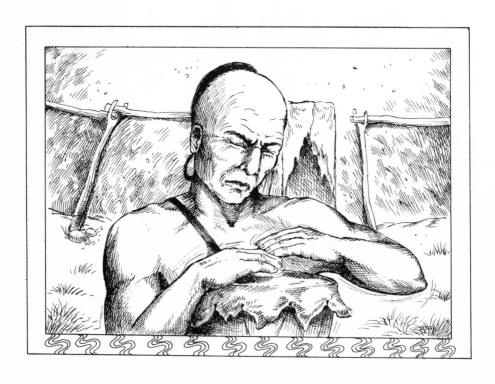

Some of the Indian men hurried to get their
weapons and food.
One of the young Indians decided he would go.
He had never been on the warpath.
He wanted to fight the enemy.
He was not afraid!
He would not run away!
Now was the time.
He ran to tell his parents.

Other warriors did not want to fight.
They sat inside the council house
and smoked and talked of war.
The women went back to their gardens.
Others went to hoe weeds in the fields.
The planting of corn would soon begin.
The fields must be ready.

18

The chieftain waited outside his winter house.
Inside a fire burned on the stone hearth
in the center of the earth floor.
Around the hearth were two circles
of benches covered with skins.
One circle was higher than the other.
One by one the warriors came and stood
by the chieftain, who welcomed them.
The men brought bows of hickory wood.

The bow strings were of twisted bear gut.
The braves had skin quivers.
In the quivers were long arrows.
Some arrow points were made of stone.
Other points were made from deer antlers.
Many warriors brought long pointed spears.
Others had wooden clubs and shields
of reed cane.
The clubs were edged with rows
of jagged stone points.
All the Indians had skin pouches filled
with corn meal.
Corn meal was the only food a man on the
warpath was allowed to eat.
But it was enough.
Corn was a very nourishing food.

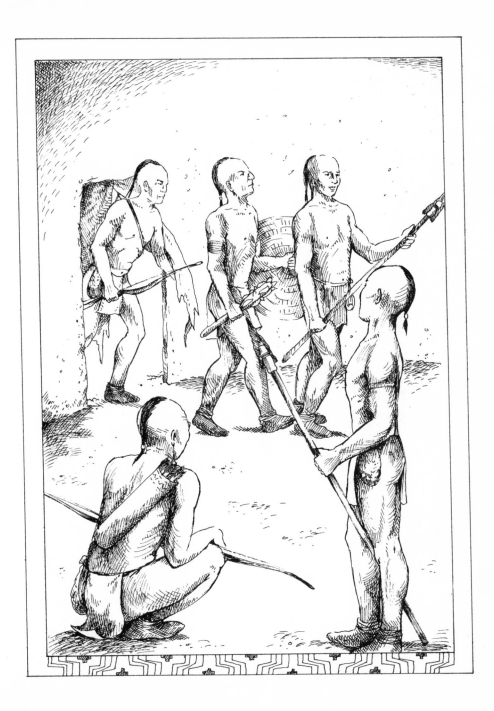

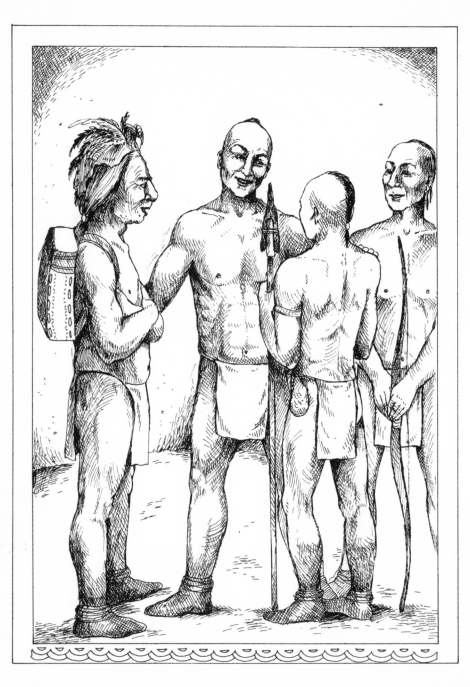

The chieftain and the other warriors greeted
the new young warrior warmly.
A priest joined the group.
He had a small wooden chest strapped
to his back.
This was the sacred ark.
In it were holy vessels and magic objects.
The holy ark would give the warriors
power and strength.
Only the priest and chief could
carry it into battle.
It was not allowed to touch the ground
and was guarded at all times.

Ten warriors had gathered.
The chieftain led them through the low doorway
of his winter house.
Then skins were placed across the door.
The Indians sat on benches.
The young warrior sat near the fire.
He wanted to see and hear everything that
happened as they all prepared for battle.
The priest placed the sacred ark on a stone
near the fire.
He placed a clay pot filled with water on the fire
and cut slices of a plant called button snakeroot.
He dropped them into the pot.
When the water boiled, the priest
opened the ark.
From it he took some sacred bowls
and poured the war medicine
of snakeroot into them.

He handed the first bowl to the
new young warrior.
The warrior drank.
The drink was bitter and hot,
but it would wash away the evil inside him.
To go to war, he must be pure
in body and in mind.
The sacred vessels of the bitter drink were
passed to all the other braves.
For three days the men of the war party
cleansed themselves with the war medicine.

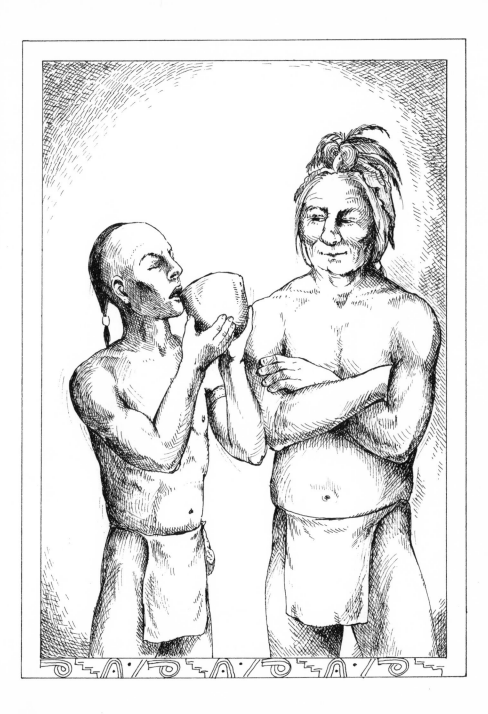

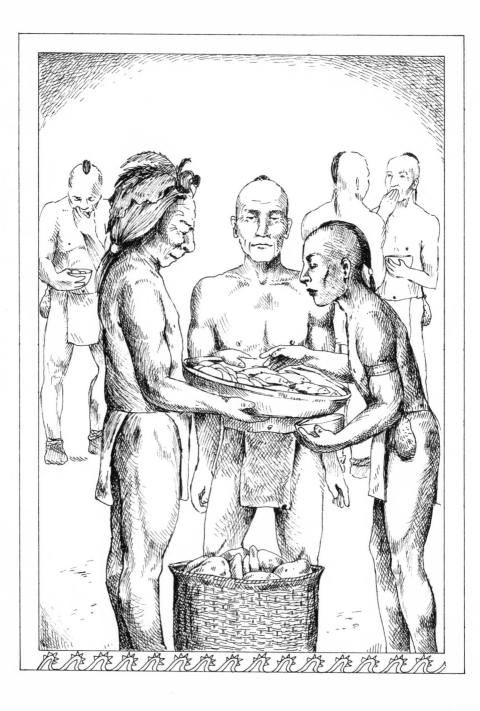

They were not allowed to eat during the day,
but each day at sunset the priest brought food,
and the warriors ate all they wanted.
The old warriors told of their adventures
in earlier wars.
The young warrior listened carefully
to what they said.
He heard much about fighting
and much about their enemy.

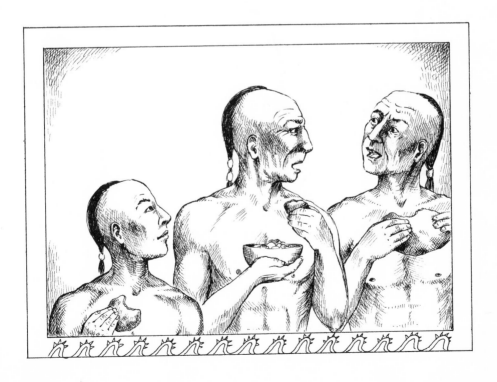

On the third day the war party was ready
to leave the winter house.
They had fasted to help their courage.
They had cleansed themselves with the sacred
drink of snakeroot.
They were ready to meet the enemy in battle.
Each warrior wore a breechclout about his waist
and skin moccasins on his feet.
His face and body were painted in his own
designs of red and black.
Red was the color of power and triumph.
Black was the symbol of death.

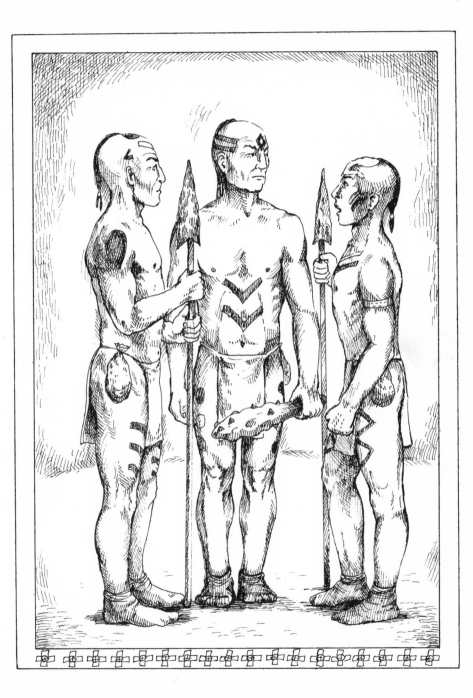

The chieftain led them from the winter house.
He sang a song of war.
The priest came next,
the sacred ark strapped to his back.
The braves followed in a single line.
They gave the war cry as they walked.
"Whoo whoop! Whoo whoop!"

They walked through the town,
their painted faces and bodies terrible to see.
They shook their weapons fiercely.
The villagers came from their houses to watch.
They hoped the war party would safely return.
They called out encouragement to the new
young warrior, who marched proudly.

He prayed to his gods for help.
He wanted to be brave in battle.
Already he could hear in his mind
his shouts insulting the enemy.
He could see the rush of spears
and arrows in the air.
He saw the enemy huts ablaze and smoke
filling the town.
He saw himself as he and the chieftain
drove the last of the enemy from the town.
What praise he would get for this!
What stories he would tell at the victory
dance back home!

When the war party entered the woods,
they fell silent.
They wanted to be able to hear any sounds.
They wanted to know if any danger lay ahead.

When they stopped to rest,
the warriors did not lean against the trees.
They did not sit in the shade of trees or bushes.
They did not sit on the ground in daylight.
Instead they sat on rocks or logs.
These were the rules of their gods.
The gods would grant them favor in battle
if they followed all the rules.
That was why they had fasted
and drunk the snakeroot medicine.
The sacred ark was always placed
on a stone or a log.
Sometimes the ark was carried by the chieftain,
but most of the time by the priest.
Only the priest was allowed to offer the warriors
food and drink.

On the second morning of the march, a brave
told of a dream he had had the night before.
A spirit had appeared and told him
he would die unless he turned back.
The chief told him to go home.
The new young brave was glad he had
had no bad dreams.

On the afternoon of the second day
the party climbed a hill.
Below them lay the town of their enemy.
In the twilight the warriors watched
the people in that town.
The cooking fires were lit.
Children played and chased dogs.
No one knew a war party was watching them.

Before daylight came on the following day
the priest woke the warriors.
From the ark he gave each one a sacred root
to chew, but told them not to swallow it.
The braves then spat it into their hands and
rubbed it over their bodies and faces.
It was a kind of magic said the priest
to protect them from enemy arrows.

The priest stayed behind to guard the ark as
the warriors followed the chieftain down the hill.
They surrounded the town.
The new young warrior shook with excitement.
He was also afraid.
Would he be brave enough to fight warriors
who had fought in many battles?
He would do his best.

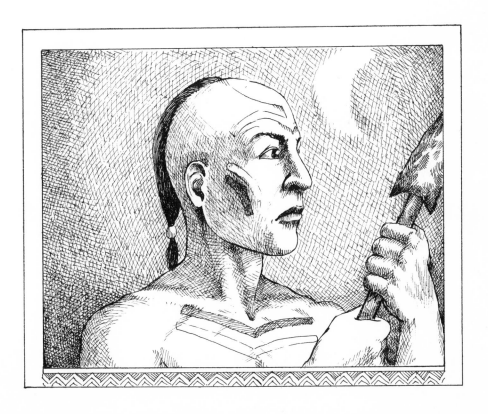

The braves strung their bows.
They waited in the darkness.
Now it grew lighter.
Suddenly the chieftain gave the war cry.
"Whoo whoop whoop!"
The warriors left their hiding places.
They shouted and rushed toward the town.
They filled the air with arrows.
They threw their long pointed spears.

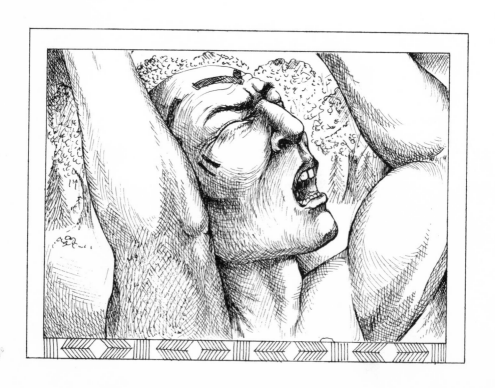

The enemy warriors ran from their houses
with their weapons.
Smoke and fire began to rise.
The young warrior shouted.

50

He shouted to give himself the courage to fight,
for now he could see the enemy.
It was a young brave who looked
very much like himself!

A spear flew through the air.
It entered the young brave's chest.
He fell to the ground and
pulled at the spear.
But he could not draw it from his body.
He screamed with pain.
The new young warrior watched,
frozen with horror.

A war club suddenly crushed his leg.
He fell, gasping.
It hurt him terribly.
The cries and noise of battle confused him.
He crawled toward a hut,
hoping to find shelter there.
Warriors fought back and forth around him.
They stepped on his broken leg.
He cried out, again and again.

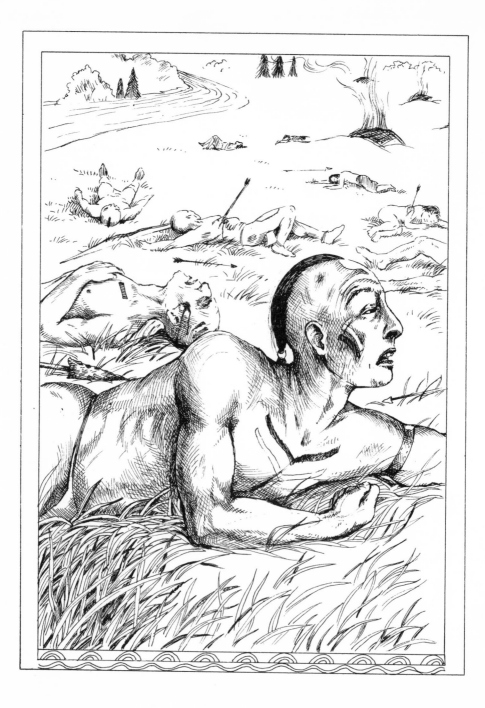

Then the war moved away from the village.
The young warrior pulled himself up.
Some friends near him were moaning.
They had bloody faces.
He saw others lying dead with arrows
sticking from their bodies.
Now he understood what battle meant.
He had never dreamed it could be like this.
Why had the chief not told him?
The chief had only talked of the glory of battle.
No one spoke of the pain and the terror.
No one told him that the enemy
was just like himself.

Now the war had ended.
His village had won the victory.
But he would not be asked to join
the victory dance,
for he had killed no one.
But the young new warrior did not care.
He looked at the dead young enemy warrior.
Who had been the bravest? he wondered.
He waited for someone to come to help him.
And he prayed that the spirits would never
send a war party from his town again.

AFTERWORD

William O. Steele has spent a lifetime studying
the early Indian people of the southeastern
section of the North American continent,
especially the rich and accretive culture of the
Cherokee. In this study of a sixteenth-century
tribe, he has attempted to re-create its life-style
through the story of a young brave who is eager
to prove himself a man. Although the Indians of
this region before the arrival of the white man
were not vastly preoccupied with warfare, the
young warriors, like youths of all races, tended
to cling to the belief that fighting in conflicts of
every kind would make them brave and honored
among their peers. This book is meant to help
dispel that belief.

GLOSSARY

ark: a square wooden box with a lid. It held
religious objects and was carried into war by a
priest.
arrowhead: a wedge-shaped stone fastened to
the end of an arrow with glue and string.
breechclout: a long, narrow strip of soft deerskin
that goes between the legs and is held in
place by a belt around the waist.
fasting: going without food. The Indians thought
this made them clean and pure and pleasing
to the gods, so that the gods would help
them.
flint: a very hard stone that can be shaped with
bone and stone tools into arrowheads, knives,
and spear points.

hearth: a large flat stone or a raised platform of clay on which food is cooked inside a building.

kin: a group of people of the same family and also those related by marriage. Kinfolks.

moccasin: a shoe made of smoked deer or elk hide.

quiver: a long round sheath closed at the bottom but open on top. It was made of animal skin and was used to carry the arrows of warriors.

sacred: religious or holy. Belonging to the gods.

spirits: invisible supernatural beings who may help or harm people.

vessel: a hollow bowl, pot, or cup that is used to hold liquids or food.

warrior: a person who is a soldier and fights battles with spears, clubs, knives, and arrows.

William O. Steele is the respected author of more than twenty-five popular books for young readers, one of which, *The Perilous Road*, was a Newbery Medal Honor Book. Noted for his vivid portrayal of the frontier period of our history, Mr. Steele travels widely, discussing his work with groups of students, teachers, and librarians. He lives with his wife, author Mary Q. Steele, on Signal Mountain in Tennessee, where they are frequently visited by their three grown-up children.

Lorinda Bryan Cauley is a gifted young artist, a graduate of the Rhode Island School of Design. She has illustrated two other books in the Let Me Read series: *Bill Pickett: First Black Rodeo Star* and *Curley Cat Baby-Sits*. She and her husband Patrick, a painter and art teacher, live in Escondido, California.